KU-016-048

OXFORD BOOKWORMS LIBRARY
Thriller & Adventure

On the Edge
Stage 3 (1000 headwords)

Series Editor: Jennifer Bassett
Founder Editor: Tricia Hedge
Activities Editors: Jennifer Bassett and Christine Lindop

GILLIAN CROSS

On the Edge

Retold by
Clare West

Illustrated by
John Batten

OXFORD UNIVERSITY PRESS

Oxford University Press
Great Clarendon Street, Oxford OX2 6DP

Oxford   New York
Auckland   Bangkok   Buenos Aires   Cape Town   Chennai
Dar es Salaam   Delhi   Hong Kong   Istanbul   Karachi   Kolkata
Kuala Lumpur   Madrid   Melbourne   Mexico City   Mumbai   Nairobi
São Paulo   Shanghai   Taipei   Tokyo   Toronto

OXFORD and OXFORD ENGLISH
are trade marks of Oxford University Press

ISBN 0 19 423010 4

Original edition © Gillian Cross 1984

First published by Oxford University Press 1984

This simplified edition © Oxford University Press 2000

Third impression 2003

First published in Oxford Bookworms 1994

This second edition published in the Oxford Bookworms Library 2000

Typeset by Wyvern Typesetting Ltd, Bristol

Printed in Spain

CONTENTS

1 TUG IS TAKEN AWAY

Day One – Sunday 7th August

Tug was running. His legs ached, his feet hurt, all his body was screaming at him to stop running. But he didn't want to stop. He wanted today's run to be better and faster than ever before. Now he was nearly at the end of his run, and his legs were burning, but he still went on running. As he came round the last street corner, he saw his own front door, a hundred metres away. *I mustn't stop now!* he thought. *I promised myself I'd do eight kilometres, and I will!*

The church bells were ringing, and the blood was beating in his ears. Suddenly it all seemed easy, and his legs felt strong. *I can do it!* he said happily to himself.

His legs ached, his feet hurt . . .

1

He reached the front door, and looked at his watch. 36 minutes 20 seconds. *At last! Eight kilometres in less than 37 minutes! I've been trying to do that for weeks!*

He put his key in the door. Now he could have a hot bath. His mother would get home later. She had promised to cook him a special meal – chicken and chips, and a chocolate cake. He smiled as he pushed open the door.

Strange! The house was dark, too dark. And there was something more . . . But he was too tired to think. Suddenly there was an arm round his neck and a hand over his face. He fell, and everything went black.

Day Two – Monday 8th August

Fifteen hours later and two hundred kilometres away in Derbyshire, Jinny Slattery came out of the farmhouse. In the moonlight she could see the ridge of mountains called Ashdale Great Edge. It stood, black and frightening, against the sky, with the Castle Rock at its southern end.

Jinny walked away from the farmhouse, and took the narrow road up the hill. It was two o'clock in the morning, and very quiet. When she reached some trees, her father stepped out and touched her arm.

'Oh!' she cried in surprise, and felt angry with herself. He had told her to be quiet.

'Follow me,' Joe said, and went on up the road. He walked quickly and silently, his dog just behind him.

I must remember what he told me to do, Jinny thought.

I don't want to make a mistake!

Now they were high up on the moors. Further along was an old cottage, which Mrs Hollins used to rent to summer visitors. It was almost hidden by trees. On the right was a gate into a field, the field which they had chosen.

Jinny felt sick. She knew what would happen next. Joe had already filled every hole in the hedges round the field, so the gate was the only way out. Now he was putting a net over the gate.

The cottage was almost hidden by trees.

3

Just then they heard a car driving up the road.

'Where is it going?' asked Jinny. 'This road only goes to the moors and Mrs Hollins' cottage.'

'Visitors,' said Joe softly, 'probably renting the cottage. Keep quiet, they won't see us in the dark.'

The car drove slowly past them and stopped in front of the cottage. Jinny could hear the voices of a man and a woman, and then a strange noise. Were they pulling something heavy into the house? She couldn't see what was happening.

When it was quiet again, Joe said softly, 'Remember, Jinny. Remember everything I told you,' and went silently into the field, followed by his dog.

Jinny was shaking now, not from cold but from fear and excitement. She knew that Joe and the dog were moving slowly through the field. She thought of the hare, lying asleep in the grass. It would try to escape through the gate. Then she must do what Joe had told her.

I can't! she thought. But she had to do it. 'If you want to eat meat, you must be able to kill an animal,' Joe had said. 'Why should other people do it for you?'

But in the end it almost seemed easy. The hare tried to jump through the gate and was caught in the net. Automatically Jinny hit its neck hard, and the hare's warm dead body fell at her feet. As she was looking at it, Joe arrived. 'Good girl,' he said, and started taking the net off the gate.

Just then a loud noise broke the silence. It was the sound

4

The hare was caught in the net.

of hammering, and it came from the cottage.

'What's that?' Jinny cried. But Joe didn't stop what he was doing. 'Nothing to do with us,' he replied. That was what he always said. For him the Slattery family was much more important than the outside world.

'But if someone hears,' said Jinny, 'they'll come up here to see, and then the police will catch us . . . stealing hares that don't belong to us!'

'Don't worry,' said Joe calmly. 'From the village you can't hear anything that happens up here. We'll make sure that we get home with the hare before anyone comes.'

They walked down the road to the farmhouse. *I'm not like Joe,* thought Jinny. *I always want to know why things happen. And I want to know what's happening in that cottage!*

10.00 a.m.

Seven hours later, Tug woke up in the cottage. The room was full of sunshine and very loud music. Above him was a

There was a high window, with strong bars across it.

high window, with strong bars across it, and blue sky outside.

It must be a dream. He wanted to wake up, and find himself in his own bedroom. But the dream did not go away.

Suddenly he noticed a woman at the door. She was about thirty, and very thin, with long legs, long brown hair and long fingers. But her eyes were the most interesting thing about her. They were large and yellow-brown, almost golden.

She said something, but he couldn't hear her because of the music. 'Sorry, I didn't hear that,' he said.

'I *said* how are you *feeling*?' she shouted angrily.

6

Tug tried to sit up. When he moved his head, he felt sick. 'What happened?' he asked. 'I don't remember this place.' He was sure he had never been there before.

The woman sounded careless, unworried. 'You fell . . . hit your head . . . we had to carry you upstairs . . .'

It was *important*, but he couldn't hear because the music was so loud. 'It's too noisy! We can't talk!' he shouted.

She didn't answer, but opened the bedroom door and shouted to someone. The music was louder through the open door. Tug couldn't think, and his head was still hurting.

A man came into the room, with slow, unhurried steps. He had a strangely white face, with cold blue eyes and thick black hair. The woman spoke quietly to him. Tug couldn't hear.

'Look,' said Tug. He wanted to sound as polite as possible. 'I don't remember anything. Where am I? And how did I get here? And who are you? *Please will you tell me what's happening?*'

'Don't worry,' said the man coldly. 'You hit your head and you've forgotten a few things. That's all. You'll be fine after a rest.'

He turned to go, but Tug reached out for his arm.

'Please!' he cried wildly. 'You must tell me *something*!'

'We're in the cottage that we've rented for our holiday, in the north of England. You remember? Now try and sleep.'

'But who are you?' shouted Tug. They were both leaving

the room. The man said something that Tug didn't hear, '. . . mirror . . .' and closed the door behind him. Tug jumped out of bed and ran to the door, but it was locked.

Suddenly he felt very cold. The music still filled his head, but it didn't stop him thinking now. He had hoped this was all a mistake, that they would answer his questions and explain everything, or take him home. But now he realized that they wanted to keep him a prisoner in that room.

It was a small room just under the roof, with only a bed and a cupboard in it. He looked up at the window above his head. They had hammered the bars on to it very recently. He couldn't escape that way. He sat on the bed and put his head in his hands. He had never felt so miserable and frightened before. Just then he thought of his mother. He knew what she would say to him now. *Why do you always feel sorry for yourself? Get up and do something!* He felt better when he thought of her small angry face. *Cheer up, Tug!* he told himself, and got up to look in the cupboard.

He was very pleased to find his clothes there, all ready for him to wear. But as he reached for them, he noticed something. On the inside of the door was a long mirror. What had the man said? *Something about a mirror.* Slowly Tug turned to look at himself.

And for a second he was in a bad dream. Because the face in the mirror was not his. Then he realized what was different – his hair. It was *black*, not fair. His face seemed very white, and his blue eyes looked coldly back at him. He looked at himself in the mirror for a long time. With the

Slowly Tug turned to look at himself.

black hair, white face and cold blue eyes, he looked just like the man. He could almost be his son.

12.45 p.m.

Jinny ran into the village. Her father had asked her to post something, so she wanted to get to the post office before it closed for lunch. Outside the post office she saw Rachel Hollins sitting on a wall. Rachel's father was the village policeman, and her mother worked in the post office. Rachel was very pretty, and always wore beautiful clothes.

'Hello Jinny!' she cried. 'Do you like my new dress?'

'Very nice,' replied Jinny crossly. 'But I couldn't wear that for working on the farm.'

'Oh, I forgot!' said Rachel. She smiled sweetly – too sweetly, and Jinny wanted to hit her. 'I'm so sorry! Poor

Jinny! You have to work so hard and you never have any new clothes and . . .' She stopped as she saw someone behind Jinny. 'I must go in and have lunch,' she said quickly, and ran inside.

Jinny turned to see who was behind her. It was a woman, with the strangest, loveliest eyes she had ever seen – big, yellow-brown eyes, almost golden. *Hare's eyes*, thought Jinny. The woman looked like a hare, with her long legs and thin face.

'I can see that girl only thinks about clothes,' said the Hare-woman to Jinny, and walked into the post office. Jinny watched her go. *What an interesting woman!* she thought. *And she understands about Rachel!*

Inside the post office the one o'clock news was on the radio. The Hare-woman, Mrs Hollins, and Jinny all listened.

Terrorists are holding thirteen-year-old Liam Shakespeare, Harriet Shakespeare's son, at the family home in London. Police are trying to—

'How terrible!' said Mrs Hollins. 'That poor boy!'

'Who's Harriet Shakespeare?' asked Jinny.

'You haven't heard of her?' asked the Hare-woman in surprise. 'She's a television reporter, always looking for other people's secrets. Thinks herself very important.'

Mrs Hollins pretended to feel sorry for Jinny. 'Poor girl, she doesn't have any newspapers or radio or television in her house,' she explained. 'Her family grow their own food, make their own clothes. They never buy anything new!'

10

Mrs Hollins always laughs at us Slatterys, thought Jinny. 'We prefer to do everything for ourselves,' she said. She really wanted the stranger to understand.

But Mrs Hollins had started talking about the news again. 'That poor Harriet Shakespeare! She must be very worried. A mother always worries about her children. Have *you* any children?' she asked the Hare-woman.

'Ye–es, yes, I have. A son, Philip, almost fourteen.'

'Well, well! My daughter Rachel and Jinny here are both nearly fourteen. Are you staying near here?'

The Hare-woman laughed. 'Well, yes, we're staying in your cottage. We arrived late last night.'

The woman looked like a hare, with her long legs and thin face.

11

'Oh, you're Mrs *Doyle*!' Mrs Hollins said, and shook the stranger's hand warmly. *So the Hare-woman was one of the visitors to the cottage!* thought Jinny.

'In fact, I hope we didn't wake everyone in the village up last night,' said the Hare-woman. 'Philip fell over and crashed into some furniture. There was a terrible noise. He hit his head, so he'll be in bed for a while.'

Jinny said nothing, but she knew that wasn't true.

'We were very tired,' continued the Hare-woman, 'so we took Philip upstairs and went to bed immediately.'

Another lie! thought Jinny. *You didn't go to bed immediately. You hammered and hammered. Why are you lying?*

Suddenly the Hare-woman seemed to remember something. She stopped talking, bought some food and hurried out.

Jinny walked slowly back to the farm. At first she had liked the stranger, with her beautiful honest eyes. But *why* was she lying?

2   WHAT'S HAPPENING AT THE COTTAGE?
Day Three – Tuesday 9th August

8.00 a.m.

Tug was lying on the bed. He hadn't slept since the Man and the Woman walked out after their first visit, hours ago. The music had a strong beat which hammered at the inside of his head, and it hadn't stopped all night. He was very tired, and hungry and thirsty. But he was watching the door and waiting for Them.

When the door opened, the music was louder for a moment as the Man entered. He looked at Tug.

'Did you sleep well?' he asked, after a moment.

'No,' said Tug. 'I – I'm thirsty.'

'Have some water,' answered the Man. 'I've brought some.' And he offered Tug a glass of water.

I'm not taking anything from you, Tug wanted to say, *before you tell me what's happening.* But he was so thirsty! He took the glass and drank all the water. Then he turned to the Man and said, 'Tell me—'

'Sit down on the bed,' ordered the Man.

Something in the Man's face told Tug that it was not a good idea to refuse. He sat down. The Man opened the door and, while watching Tug carefully, put his arm outside. And suddenly the music stopped.

Tug fell back on the bed, free from the terrible noise at last. The room was beautifully silent.

Then he heard someone climbing the stairs. The Woman walked in. She was carrying a tray.

'Breakfast,' she said. 'Look.' It was a dream breakfast. A big plate of fried eggs, tomatoes and bread, with a cup of hot, strong tea.

Tug could not stop looking at the tray. But the Woman did not move. She stayed near the door.

'Well?' he said at last. 'Isn't it for me?'

13

'Oh yes,' she replied. 'It's for you. But what do you say first?'

I'm not a child! thought Tug angrily. *She's teaching me to be polite!* But he was very hungry.

'Thank you,' he said.

'Thank you – what?' she asked.

'I don't understand,' said Tug. *Is this a game?*

'You usually call her something,' said the Man.

Tug began to see what they wanted. *Were they serious?* He pretended that he still didn't understand.

'What do you mean? *What* do I usually call her?'

It was the Woman who answered. 'You usually call me Ma. And your breakfast will be cold soon.'

But Tug wasn't ready to do what they wanted yet. He turned to the Man. 'And I suppose I call you Dad!'

'No,' smiled the Man calmly. 'You could, but you don't. You call me Doyle.'

Doyle . . . Ma . . . Tug looked from one to the other. It almost seemed true. Suddenly he shouted, 'You're crazy! All that's rubbish! Why don't you explain what's happening . . .'

The door banged shut. The Woman had walked out and taken his breakfast with her.

'That was stupid of you,' said Doyle. 'She's angry with you. Mothers are like that sometimes, aren't they?'

'But—' said Tug, and stopped. He could hear her climbing up the stairs again.

'Now be careful this time,' said Doyle quietly.

14

The Woman entered again, with the tray. Tug could smell the hot food. It looked wonderful.

'Breakfast,' said the Woman, for the second time.

Tug could smell the hot food.

What does it matter? thought Tug. *Ma isn't what I call my mother. I call her Hank.*

'Thank you – Ma,' he said. The Woman gave him the tray, and left the room. As Doyle followed her, he turned and smiled slowly at Tug. 'Have a good breakfast – Philip.'

'I'm *not* Philip!' Tug shouted. 'And you're *not* my parents!' But the door had already closed.

And then the music started. With that terrible beat in his head, he wasn't sure of anything any more.

10.00 a.m.

Jinny was digging in the garden. While she was working, she was talking angrily to herself. *Forget it! It's nothing to do with you!* But she couldn't stop herself thinking of the Hare woman. Why had she lied about the noises in the night? And why had there been so much hammering at the cottage?

Suddenly she had an idea. She could go up to the cottage *now*. She knew that she should go on with her work – there were always lots of jobs to do on the Slatterys' small farm – but she really wanted to understand the mystery. Perhaps the Hare-woman had a good reason for lying and perhaps she would tell Jinny all about it . . .

Soon she was walking up the narrow road to the moors. The cottage was on the left, but she didn't go up to it. She climbed up the small hill behind the house, and hid in the trees halfway up the hill. She couldn't see anybody in the cottage, but she could hear a radio playing loud music.

16

Something was different about the cottage . . . Jinny went a few steps nearer, to look more closely at the window in the roof . . .

Suddenly a voice spoke from below. 'Hallo.'

'Oh!' cried Jinny in surprise, and the branch that she was holding broke. She fell, and slid all the way down the hill to the cottage garden.

'Well, well!' said the voice. Jinny looked up. It was a man with black hair and cold blue eyes. He looked angry.

Jinny thought fast. 'I – I'm sorry, I didn't mean to – You see, I was looking for – for – mushrooms.' *Would he believe her?* She continued quickly, 'They're very good to eat, er, fried in butter, for breakfast—'

'I was looking for – for – mushrooms,' Jinny said.

17

'Yes.' The cold voice stopped her. 'But perhaps you'd like to find a different place to look for mushrooms. We're here on holiday, you see, and we don't want people crashing in through the kitchen window.' He was holding her by the arm as he spoke, and pulling her away from the cottage. Jinny was frightened.

Just then she heard a single wild shout from inside the cottage, followed immediately by a crashing sound. The loud music went on playing. The man shouted towards the house, 'Oh, be quiet, Philip!' *He's pretending to be a father who's angry with his son*, thought Jinny, *but I don't believe him! Why is he so cold and unfriendly? Is he hiding something?*

But she was shaking a little after her fall, and she was still afraid of the man. So she pulled her arm away, and said quickly, 'I – I must go home.' She knew that he was watching her as she hurried away from the cottage.

10.30 a.m.

The music was still playing in the bedroom. Tug had just finished his breakfast when he heard the noise of Jinny's fall outside. He jumped on to the bed and looked out of the window. He could only see the sky and the tops of trees, but he heard a girl saying, 'They're very good to eat, fried in butter, for breakfast—' *Who was she? Could he send her a message? Would it be dangerous?* Then he heard feet running up the stairs. It was now or never. He pushed open the window and shouted as loudly as possible, 'Help!'

18

The next moment the Woman had crashed into him. He fell on to the floor, and she held him down with one strong hand over his mouth. She only let him get up when she heard the Man come back into the house.

'*Right!*' she said. '*Now* you learn to obey orders!' She hit him hard across the face, on one side and then the other. She went on hitting him, in time to the beat of the music. Tug began to think that she would never stop. He was trying hard not to scream, because when he started, he would go on and on, like her . . . Then suddenly Doyle was there. He put a finger on the Woman's arm. Just one finger. And no words. But it was enough. She stopped.

'Stupid woman,' said Doyle calmly. 'Stupid to hit his *face*. Get some water.' She went downstairs.

'She hit me,' said Tug. 'Just because I—'

'You have to understand,' Doyle said quietly. 'We'll kill you if we have to.'

The room seemed very quiet, although the music was still playing. *I've never been really afraid before*, thought Tug. He was full of a deep, cold fear. For the first time in his life, he realized that he could die. Not in a hundred years, or when he was very old, but now. Today or tomorrow.

But the moment passed. Soon Doyle and the Woman were washing Tug's face, like careful parents. When the Woman left the room, Doyle sat by the door. Now he had a gun with him, which he was cleaning. Tug could not take his eyes off the cold grey gun. *Perhaps he's going to kill me now . . . to shoot me with the gun . . .*

19

Doyle sat by the door, cleaning his gun.

At last Doyle put the gun down. Suddenly angry, Tug shouted, 'How can you two pretend to be my parents? Look what that woman did to my face! She can't be my mother!'

'Most murders happen in the family, you know. Your family are the people who can give you most pain. They know how to hurt you. Parents are the worst.'

20

'Then why are *you* trying to hurt me?' asked Tug.

'Trying to hurt you? No, Philip, we're doing our best for you. But we're prisoners of the family ourselves. Like the rest of the world.'

And he smiled as he picked up his gun again.

11.00 a.m.

Jinny was still running when she reached the village. *I must tell Keith what's happening at the cottage! I know he'll listen to me!* Keith was Rachel Hollins' brother, and Jinny's best friend in the village, although he was five years older than her.

She found him in the Hollins' sitting-room, with a lot of different newspapers in front of him.

'*Keith!*' she cried. 'I've got to tell you! It was so awful! I didn't do anything wrong but he—'

She began to cry as she started speaking. But Keith always took care of her. He gave her his cup of tea.

'Now, drink that, Jinny,' he told her. 'You'll feel better in a moment. Then tell me all about it.'

She told him about the people at the cottage, and explained how the Hare-woman had told lies in Mrs Hollins' shop. 'So I went to the cottage to see,' she continued. 'And I slid down the hill behind the house – and there was an awful man who told me to go away. But the *really important* thing is what I heard!'

'Tell me quickly, or I'll die of excitement.' Keith was laughing quietly to himself.

'*Listen*,' she said angrily. 'It's *serious. I heard someone shouting "Help!"* And the person who shouted meant it. Now what do you think, Keith?'

'Well,' said Keith, after thinking for a moment. 'Perhaps someone was just playing a game.'

'A game! No! There was hammering – and she told lies – and I heard the shout! These are facts!'

'These newspapers have all got facts in,' said Keith. 'But they make different stories out of the same facts. That's my school work for the summer – to take a story and follow it in all the newspapers for a week, to see how different the stories are, although the facts are the same. Can you think of a story that I could follow?'

Jinny remembered the Hare-woman in the shop, listening to the radio. 'You could do the story of Harriet Shakespeare's son, you know, held by terrorists. But Keith, you're forgetting *my* story! What about the voice that shouted "Help!"? What can I do?'

'I agree it *is* a bit strange. But there's probably a good reason for it. If you find some more *facts*, I'll ask my father to investigate it. But now I really must start reading these newspapers. Sorry I can't help.'

I'll investigate it myself, thought Jinny crossly.

Day Four – Wednesday 10th August

11.00 a.m.

Tug felt terrible. The music had given him a headache. He

22

was alone for a moment, while Doyle and the Woman were downstairs. He looked tiredly round the room, at the cupboard, the walls, the wallpaper . . . An idea suddenly came to him. *If I tear a piece of paper off the wall behind the cupboard, nobody will notice . . .* He pulled at a corner of the paper. *Hurry, hurry! One of Them will be back soon.* Now he had a large piece of paper in his hand. With the pencil that he always kept in his pocket, he wrote a few words quickly on the paper. Then, with his hands shaking, he folded the paper into the shape of a dart. *Hurry, hurry!* He jumped on to the bed, pushed his arm through the bars, and threw the dart as far as possible out of the open window. *That's your only chance to get a message to the outside world,* he told himself. *I hope that someone finds it soon!*

He threw the dart as far as possible out of the open window.

23

3 FREE PEOPLE

Day Five – Thursday 11th August

6.30 a.m.

As Jinny did her work on the farm, she could not stop thinking about the mystery of the Hare-woman and her son. She was hoping to go back to the cottage today. But at breakfast her father said, 'You'll have to make the butter today, Jinny, because your mother is making the bread. Oz,' he said to Jinny's young brother, 'you're coming to help me mend the walls round the south field. And Jinny, you'll have to plant the vegetables as well. I think you'll have time. There's a lot to do before harvest next week.'

Thanks a lot! Jinny thought angrily. *Don't I get any time for myself? It's always the same!*

Later she talked to her mother, Bella, about it.

'Mum, why do I have to spend all my time working on the farm? It's the summer holidays now. My school friends all get up late and go riding. Or shopping, like Rachel.'

'Jinny, you know why we decided to leave London and buy this farm. Joe was working much too hard in London. His work was making him ill. We wanted a healthier, freer life. I agree that it's hard work, but we *chose* this life.'

'You *two* chose it, you mean. No one asked me.'

'All children get the life that their parents have chosen. You can choose your own life when you're old enough.'

'But I want some time *now!* I'm – I'm so angry with Dad! He gives me too much work to do. Sometimes I – I almost

24

want to kill him!'

Her mother did not reply immediately. Then she said quietly, 'It's because you love him that you want to kill him. But it's the wrong answer. If you kill the people who you

'But I want some time now!' *said Jinny.*

love, or run away from them, you only destroy yourself in the end. You have to accept them, or change yourself.'

Suddenly Jinny realized that it was true. Accepting what other people wanted, and working together – that was family life. She smiled at her mother.

5.30 p.m.

Doyle looked at his watch. 'Time to go downstairs.'

'What?' said Tug. He had been there for almost five days now. Was it *possible* to leave the room?

Doyle pushed him towards the door, and they went down the stairs. At the same moment Doyle turned off the music. For the last two days it had not stopped for a second. Now, the house was suddenly silent, and Tug felt frightened.

They were in a big sitting-room, full of old heavy furniture. The Woman was sitting in an armchair.

'Sit down,' she said to Tug. 'We're going to have a nice family evening in front of the television.'

Clearly, Tug's visit downstairs was planned. The television news was just starting.

Of course! thought Tug. *I'll be in the news!*

'Good evening. The terrorists who are holding thirteen-year-old Liam Shakespeare at his home in London have said that they belong to "Free People". That is the revolutionary group which wants to end family life. They say that they want all children and adults to live free from the prison of the family.'

What's happening? thought Tug. *Am I crazy? How can*

26

I be here and in London?

'Our reporter spoke to Liam's mother, Harriet Shakespeare, at a friend's house today.'

There was Hank. Her small face looked tired, and Tug could see that she was trying not to cry. *Hank, Hank, come and save me from these people!*

'Mrs Shakespeare, have you spoken to your son?' asked the reporter.

'No,' replied Hank. 'But we can see him moving around in the house, so we know he's still alive.'

'Why do you think this group has taken your son?'

'Well, I suppose that it's because I've investigated Free People in the past. It's my job to investigate revolutionary groups.'

The television news was just starting.

'You have always said that nobody should give terrorist groups what they want. Do you still think that, now that your own son is in danger?'

'Yes, I do. But we – we don't know yet what the group wants. We'll have to wait and see.'

That's a lie! Tug thought. He always knew when Hank was lying. But she seemed to believe that he was held by terrorists in London. And the reporters believed it too.

Doyle and the Woman were watching him carefully.

'It's interesting to hear about your friend Liam, isn't it?' Doyle said slowly.

'He isn't my *friend*—' began Tug. Then he stopped. He remembered Hank saying, *We can see him moving around.* Suddenly he felt very tired. *Who am I? Where's home?* In the bedroom, with the music, he would feel better. He stood up.

'I want to go back upstairs.'

Doyle put an arm round Tug, and led him upstairs like a small child.

8.00 p.m.

Keith was very excited about the Liam Shakespeare story.

'Don't you think it's strange?' he asked Jinny.

'What do you mean?' she answered. She was very tired after a long day on the farm.

'Well, I've just shown you all the newspapers and the video of the six o'clock news. There's Harriet Shakespeare, a brave, loving mother, worried about her son. A picture of

28

mother-love and happy families. But it's the wrong picture, isn't it? The terrorists have made a bad mistake.'

Jinny was too tired to think clearly. 'What do they care? They just want money or something, don't they?'

Keith was very excited about the Liam Shakespeare story.

'Don't you understand? Terrorists aren't strong enough to change the world by themselves. So they try to make pictures that will change people's ideas. The Free People group want publicity. And in this Shakespeare story, they're making a picture that says *Mothers are wonderful*. But they don't want to say that. They want to say *Destroy family life*, because it's bad for you. Their message to the world here' – he picked up one of the papers – 'is that everybody – women, men, and children – should escape from the prison of the family. So why are they giving us the wrong message? Yes, it's a very interesting story, Jinny! What's going to happen?'

Day Six – Friday 12th August

2.00 a.m.

Tug woke up suddenly from a bad dream. The room was very dark, and a large shadow was standing over his bed. Tug screamed. A hand covered his mouth.

'Quiet,' said a voice, very softly. 'Daddy's going to tell you a bedtime story. When *I* was a small boy, *I* used to wake up in the night and cry. Because I was afraid of the dark, you see. Like you. Crying in the dark.'

'Daddy's going to tell you a bedtime story.'

Tug wanted to say, *I wasn't crying*. But he was too frightened to speak. Doyle went on. 'And when I started crying, my Daddy used to come. And he always used to hit me. So I learnt never, *never* to cry in the dark, because my Daddy didn't like it. And you know, I've inherited that from my father. I don't like my son crying in the dark.'

Tug was suddenly very angry. 'But *I* haven't inherited anything from *you*! You're not my father!'

Doyle did not seem to hear. 'That's the worst thing about families. Because my father hit me, I'll hit you, and you'll hit your children. This will go on and on—'

'No! No!' shouted Tug. 'You're not my father!'

Suddenly the light went on, and the Woman stood at the door. 'What's happening?' she asked angrily.

'I'm just telling him a little story about family life.' Doyle smiled slowly.

The Woman looked at Tug's white, frightened face. 'Come downstairs with me,' she said. 'I'll make you a hot drink.'

In the kitchen Tug said, his voice shaking, 'I didn't – didn't know Doyle was like that.'

The Woman laughed. 'Doyle doesn't often get angry, like me. But he's a very dangerous man.' For a moment she put her warm hands round Tug's, and he felt like a small child again. The fear began to disappear.

'Ma, what's going on? I just don't understand.'

She put a gentle hand on his head. 'I know it's difficult, but it'll be all right in the end. Come on now, back to bed.'

When he was in bed again, Tug suddenly realized a terrible thing. *I called her Ma.* And it was worse than that. In the kitchen he had actually felt that she was kind and loving, and could be his mother. *Was he Philip? Or Liam? And hadn't anyone found his message?*

6.30 p.m.

Jinny and her brother Oz were sitting in the Hollins' sitting-room. On the table in front of them was the dart that Tug had thrown out of the window. Keith and Mr Hollins were listening to Jinny's excited story.

'You see, Mr Hollins, Oz and I were picking mushrooms up on the moors near the cottage. We were – well, we were interested in the visitors there, so we hid in the trees near their garden. We couldn't see anything, so we were just leaving when Oz found this piece of paper on the grass! Look! It says, HELP I AM A PRISONER HERE.'

'I can read, Jinny,' said Mr Hollins, smiling. 'Well, what do you want me to do about it?'

'She wants you to go and investigate, Dad,' said Keith. 'There's something very strange about those visitors.'

'All right then,' said the policeman. 'You come with me, Jinny. We'll take the police car, drive to the cottage and just ask a few questions. Oz and Keith can stay here.'

When they arrived at the cottage, the Hare-woman opened the door. She did not seem surprised at all.

'Good evening, Mrs Doyle,' said Mr Hollins. 'Could we come in for a moment?'

'Of course.' They went straight into the sitting-room. There were books, maps and a camera on the table. *A family on holiday*, thought Jinny. There was the man with the cold blue eyes, and sitting next to him, a boy with black hair and very serious ice-blue eyes.

'This is my husband,' said the Hare-woman, 'and my son

Philip.' *They look so alike!* thought Jinny.

Mr Hollins was talking about a lost dog. 'We think that perhaps it came up here on the moors,' he said.

'There's no dog here,' smiled the man. 'But would you like to look round the house while you're here?'

'There's no dog here,' smiled the man.

'Good idea,' said Mr Hollins. 'Thank you.'

'I'll come with you,' said the Hare-woman. They went upstairs.

Jinny looked at the boy. He was staring at her, and his face was very white.

'Talk to the girl, Philip,' said his father.

The boy's voice sounded strangely polite. He was not smiling. 'Where do you live?' he asked.

'Outside the village, on a small farm . . .' Jinny was

33

talking quickly, although the boy did not seem interested. And then it happened. As Mr Hollins and the Hare-woman came downstairs, the man's eyes looked away from Jinny and the boy for a moment. In that second, while Jinny was talking, the boy stared straight at her and made the shape of a word with his mouth. *Help*.

'We must go, Jinny,' said Mr Hollins. 'Thank you, Mrs Doyle. Sorry to take up your time.'

In the car, as they drove back to the village, he explained kindly to Jinny, 'Of course you couldn't know, but the boy's a bit strange. He's nearly fourteen, but he's like a five-year-old child really. His mother told me all about it, so you see, there's nothing to investigate.'

7.15 p.m.

Tug watched the police car drive away. He hadn't been brave enough to scream for help, because of the gun in Doyle's pocket. And what had the girl and the policeman seen? The Doyle family. *But I am Tug*, he said angrily to himself. *I'm not Philip Doyle.*

'Well, we *are* a happy family,' said Doyle, smiling.

'No!' cried Tug. 'It's a lie!'

'Of course it's a lie,' agreed the Woman. 'The *idea* of the happy family is a lie. The family is a prison. We want people to escape from it.'

'I didn't mean that rubbish!' cried Tug. 'I meant—'

'Oh Tug!' she said. 'Don't you understand?'

Tug had been afraid of Doyle's gun, but he was much

more afraid now. 'What did you *call* me?'

'What? Oh, I called you Tug. Don't you remember? It's the name that I called you when you were a baby.'

'No,' said Tug in a low, frightened voice. It had been his secret. It was what Hank called him.

'Look.' The Woman suddenly opened her large handbag and brought out an old photo. The photo was of her when she was much younger. In her arms she was holding a small baby.

'You, six weeks old,' she said, watching Tug.

'No!' said Tug. *It can't be true!* Suddenly he took the photo, tore it into two pieces, and threw them wildly on the floor. He looked up and saw that he had really hurt the Woman. Her face was very white.

That night Tug could not sleep. *Help me, Hank*, he cried to himself. But now he could not remember Hank's face or voice. The only face he could see was long and thin, with large golden eyes. Ma's face.

4 A MESSAGE FOR HARRIET
Day Eight – Sunday 14th August

10.00 a.m.

Jinny could not forget the white, staring face of the boy at the cottage. She was busy all day on Saturday, but on Sunday, when her mother was cooking the hare for lunch, she walked down to the village to see Keith.

'Jinny, the terrorists who're holding Liam Shakespeare have said what they want!' he said excitedly.

'Who? Oh, *him*! But I want to talk to you about—'

'No, listen, this is important. They want special children's homes all over the country, where all children under sixteen can live away from their families.'

'That's crazy,' said Jinny. 'The Government will never agree to that.'

'No, of course not. But it's giving Free People some publicity for their ideas, isn't it? And they say that they'll shoot Liam if the Government don't agree by Friday.'

'Poor Harriet Shakespeare! If the terrorists are asking for something impossible, there's nothing she can do to help Liam. She must be so frightened!'

'That's the strange thing! She isn't! Last night, when I watched her on the news, she looked very calm! And guess what? She said, "I'm sure I can get Liam out by Friday!" She really did sound sure about it. Here she is on the video.'

On the television Jinny saw Harriet Shakespeare's small white face and very serious ice-blue eyes . . . ice-blue eyes . . .

'Show me the video again!' Jinny said quickly.

'Why?' asked Keith, but Jinny did not answer. They watched the video again. *It must be him!* thought Jinny. *But what will happen if I'm right?*

'Have you got a photo of Liam, from a newspaper?' she asked. *It's impossible*, she was thinking.

The photo that Keith held out to her showed the face of

the boy who was in the cottage. But in the photo his hair was fair, not black. She picked up a pencil, and carefully changed the colour of his hair to black.

'What are you *doing*?' asked Keith at last.

Jinny showed him the photo, her hands shaking with excitement. 'Liam Shakespeare isn't in that London house. He's here in Derbyshire, in your Mum's cottage!'

Jinny carefully changed the colour of the boy's hair to black.

37

10.45 a.m.

Tug's room was quiet now, because the music had stopped. He was alone with the questions in his head, the questions that he could not answer.

Doyle, the Woman, the television reporters, Hank, the girl, the policeman, and his own face in the mirror all told him that he was Philip Doyle, and that Liam Shakespeare was in a house in London. So did he really believe that they were all wrong and he was right?

Was the rest of the world crazy? Or was *he* crazy?

Just then he heard the church bells from the village, and realized that it must be Sunday. Last time he had heard them was when he was running . . .

Yes! *Last Sunday I went for a run. Hank was going to cook me a special meal . . .*

No! *Last Sunday Doyle and Ma drove me here. We're on holiday . . .*

How could he be sure which really happened? *If I can remember things about myself which are true, I can build up a picture of the real me.* He liked running. He hated bananas. He could make a cake. He could mend bicycles. He could speak some French . . .

An hour later, he was still remembering things, when the Woman came to say that lunch was ready downstairs.

When they arrived in the sitting-room, Tug was surprised to see that they were going to have a family Sunday lunch. On the big table there were knives, forks, plates and glasses, and in the centre there was a large roast chicken with a lot of different vegetables.

But Doyle did not sit down. 'Oh, very nice!' he said, with a cold smile. 'What a lovely family meal!'

'What a lovely family meal!' said Doyle, with a cold smile.

The Woman stared at him angrily. 'Don't be stupid! What does it matter? It's only a meal!'

'Nothing is *only* itself. Everything *means* something. And Sunday lunch means family life. We're against that, remember?' He turned to Tug. 'Don't look surprised, Philip. Families often argue during Sunday lunch. My parents used to argue all Sunday afternoon, and then Dad used to hit us children, again and again.'

'We don't want to hear about your past,' said the Woman.

Doyle looked coldly at her. 'It's better than hearing about *your* past, about a mother and baby—'

39

The Woman hit Doyle hard in the mouth. But before Doyle could do or say anything, Tug said quickly, 'Ma, I'm hungry.'

Doyle looked at Tug almost sadly. 'Children don't like it when their parents argue,' he said.

The Woman laughed and sat down. 'Come on, let's eat the chicken. After that we're having baked bananas.'

'Oh Ma!' cried Tug without thinking. 'You know I hate bananas. I'll be sick!'

'Of course I haven't forgotten,' she replied. 'There's an apple for you.'

1.00 p.m.

'Mr Hollins, please believe me!' cried Jinny.

'I'm sorry, Jinny,' said the policeman kindly. 'Everybody knows that Liam Shakespeare's in London. How can he be in our cottage? Now I'm going to have my lunch, so you go home and forget about it.'

Jinny and Keith walked out of the Hollins' house.

'We must do *something*!' said Jinny miserably. 'I'm really sure that it's Liam Shakespeare in the cottage.'

'And Harriet Shakespeare sounded strange on the television news, didn't she?' said Keith. 'Why was she so sure that Liam would be safe on Friday? Perhaps she *knows* that he's not in London. Listen, I've got an idea. We could send a message to her. It says in the newspaper that she's staying with a friend, Lucy Mallory. Well, if we can find Lucy Mallory's phone number, we can phone her.'

'How can we find her number?'

'Well, they've got a London street map and a London phone book at the library. I'll go there tomorrow and find the phone number. Can you meet me tomorrow evening? We'll phone Lucy Mallory together, from the village phone box.'

'All right. Shall we say – about 10 o'clock?'

Day Nine – Monday 15th August

4.00 p.m.

This time the Woman was sitting at the door of Tug's room. She kept her own gun by the side of her chair.

'Why was Doyle so angry yesterday, Ma?' Tug asked.

'Oh, you know what he's like. He wants people to understand. For years he hated his father. He believed that he was bad, because his father hated *him*. Then one day he understood. It was the happiest moment of his life.'

Did Doyle ever have happy moments? Impossible! thought Tug. 'What had he understood?' he asked.

'That it isn't *natural* for people to stay in families for years and years. People stop loving and start hating. That's what happened to me. That's why I—' She stopped suddenly, then started again. 'Governments and big business want people to live in families, because if you've got a family, you've got something to lose. You don't want to fight against the government. We've got to show people how to be free! Free to live and free to fight!'

41

She looked wonderfully tall and strong and brave, as she stood in the centre of the room and waved her arms. Tug wanted to jump up and join her. But a small voice inside his head was saying, *If a speaker excites you, be very careful. Forget the excitement, and think hard about the ideas.* It was Hank's voice. Hank was right, of course.

Then something terrible happened. He thought, *Is Hank real?* He knew that Harriet Shakespeare was real because he had seen her on television. But was she really his mother? Perhaps Hank was only an idea, a wish – the kind of mother that he would like to have, instead of Ma. Perhaps he was living in a dream world. *Crazy Philip Doyle.*

He was shaking and could not speak. The Woman noticed, and came over to put her arms round him.

'What's the matter, Tug? Everything'll be all right. After tomorrow.'

Just then Doyle entered the room, with a tray. 'What's happening?' he asked the Woman coldly. 'What a wonderful picture of motherly love!'

'I was just being a little bit kind . . .'

'And what about the gun? It's on the bed, where Philip can reach it.' He picked it up. 'That's dangerous.' He stared at the Woman – a long, cold, hard stare. After a minute she turned away, and went out of the room.

Doyle gave the tray to Tug. 'Here's your supper.'

'Thanks,' Tug said. He took the tray with hands that were still shaking.

'Thanks – what?'

'Oh.' He had forgotten. 'Thanks, Doyle.'

9.50 p.m.

Jinny hurried down the road to the village, and saw Keith waiting by the phone box.

'Come on,' he said excitedly. 'I've got the number.'

The phone rang and rang. At last a voice answered. 'What number do you want? Who do you want to speak to? What is your name? What number are you calling from?'

At last a voice answered.

43

Jinny answered all these questions. Then she asked Keith, 'What's happening?'

'The police are checking all phone calls to Mrs Shakespeare or her friends, I think.'

Then another voice. 'Lucy Mallory here.'

'Please,' said Jinny hurriedly, 'I want to speak to Harriet Shakespeare. It's important. It's about Liam.'

'Wait a moment.' The woman did not sound friendly.

Then another voice spoke, the deep voice that Jinny and Keith had heard on the television news. 'Yes?'

'You – you're Harriet Shakespeare?' asked Jinny, not sure what to say. 'I – I know where Liam is.'

'Everyone knows where Liam is.' The voice was hard.

'But he's not in your house. He's a prisoner, in my village. I've seen him. He's . . .'

'Listen!' Harriet Shakespeare said angrily. 'You're the *fourteenth* person who's phoned me at Lucy's to tell me crazy stories about Liam!'

'But you must believe me! The police up here won't believe me, and we thought, when we saw you on television, that you knew something, something that you weren't telling anybody—'

'Oh yes? And *what* do I know?' Suddenly her voice was very quiet, and worried.

'That the terrorists are only pretending to hold Liam in your house. That really he's in a different place.'

'Oh.' She sounded almost thankful, Jinny thought. Then the voice became angry again. 'Well, you're wrong about

44

that. Now please just forget it, and don't ring me again.'

The phone went dead.

'Well,' said Jinny unhappily, 'we were wrong. She didn't know anything. She didn't believe me. And she was *awful*.'

'Never mind, Jinny,' said Keith slowly. 'I agree, we were wrong about *what* she knew. But I'm sure that she was hiding *something*. What could it be?'

5   ON THE EDGE

Day Ten – Tuesday 16th August

2.55 a.m.

'Tug!' The Woman was trying to wake him. 'Tug!'

'Ma? What time is it? What's the matter?'

She spoke quietly into his ear. 'Don't speak so loudly, or you'll wake Doyle. The news is on in a moment.'

'In the middle of the night?' But Tug took the small radio from her and put it near his ear.

'Good morning. This is the news. Police have arrested the terrorists who said that they were holding Liam Shakespeare at his home in London. But when the police entered the house just before midnight, Liam himself was not there. One of the group is a boy of fifteen, with fair hair, who looks like Liam. It is not known why the terrorists were pretending to hold Liam prisoner. The police are continuing to investigate the matter.'

'I don't understand,' said Tug, still half asleep.

45

She held his hand. 'You're all right. We just have to wait, wait until the end of today.'

Today. Tuesday. 'Aren't you going to tell me—'

'No! Go to sleep now!'

But he could not sleep. He had so many things to think about. Liam Shakespeare had disappeared. So who was Tug? He tried to remember the facts that he knew about himself. He liked running. He hated bananas . . .

6.45 a.m.

Jinny was getting breakfast ready. She hadn't slept all night. She knew that she was right about the boy in the cottage. *But today I won't have time to worry about it!* she thought, *because it's our harvest day, the busiest day of the year.* All the neighbours were coming to help.

Just then she noticed a car coming up the narrow road to the farm. *A visitor! On harvest day!* It was a woman, dressed in an expensive suit, and wearing sunglasses. Jinny went out to meet her.

'You're Jinny Slattery,' the woman said. Jinny recognized the deep voice that she had heard on the phone last night. 'You gave your name and the number of the village phone box, luckily. That's how I found you. I've driven all the way from London, and the girl in the post office told me where your farm was.'

'But why have you come?' asked Jinny. 'You didn't believe me last night!'

'Haven't you heard the news? Liam isn't at our home in

London. I came to find you because you're the only person who seems to know where he is. You're my only hope! Where is he? How can I get him out?' She sounded desperate.

'Look, I can show you the house where he is, but—'

'We must hurry! There isn't much time! We've got to get him out *by 2 o'clock today!*'

'You're my only hope!' said Harriet.

7.15 a.m.

Tug knew that today was different from other days. At breakfast, both Doyle and the Woman kept their guns on the table by their hands, ready for – what? Tug felt afraid.

Their guns were on the table by their hands.

Doyle stared coldly at Tug. 'Suppose that this is the last day of your life. What would you like to do most?'

'*Doyle!*' said the Woman angrily, and put her hand on Tug's arm.

Doyle continued. 'If you don't know what you'd choose to do on the last day of your life, you don't know what's really important to you. Forget about parents and other people. Only free people know the answer to that question.'

'It's not easy to know what you want,' agreed the Woman. 'Because you need to know who you really *are*. Nothing to do with your family. Just *you*.'

48

'You think you're Liam Shakespeare,' Doyle went on. 'We say you're Philip Doyle. Without one of those names, you're nobody. And you can't answer my question, can you? You don't know who you are!'

They were both staring at him, with their wild, crazy eyes. *Why should I play their games?* thought Tug. *I'm Tug, I like running. I hate bananas . . .*

'Yes, I *do* know who I am,' he said.

Doyle seemed surprised. 'Well?' he said. 'If you're so sure, what would you do on the last day of your life?'

Tug thought for a moment. He stared out of the window at the great rocky ridge which stood high against the sky. It looked black and frightening in the early morning light.

'What's that long hill called?' he asked.

Doyle smiled. He thought that Tug could not answer his question. 'That's Ashdale Great Edge. And the rock at the end is called the Castle Rock.'

'I can tell you what I'd do on the last day of my life,' Tug said calmly. 'I'd run, all the way along Ashdale Great Edge, from this end to Castle Rock.'

'That's a stupid thing to do!' said Doyle.

But I know that's what I want, and nobody can take that away from me, thought Tug. Then he noticed the Woman looking very sadly at him. He had to ask her *the* question.

'So – is this going to be the last day of my life?'

'I think perhaps – not,' Doyle answered. 'It will be the last day of someone's life, but not yours, I think.'

7.35 a.m.

Around the breakfast table sat Jinny, Oz, their parents, Harriet, and Keith, who had just arrived.

'So, Mrs Shakespeare,' said Joe Slattery, 'you think that your son is staying in the cottage with people who are probably terrorists. You don't want to go to the police because it'll take too much time. And you want us to think of a plan to save your son before two o'clock today. On harvest day, the most important day of the year for us.'

Harriet stared desperately at Joe. 'Yes,' she said.

Joe thought for a moment. 'Well, Keith here says that one of the Doyles goes to the post office to get a newspaper every day. That'll give us about twenty minutes. We can send Jinny to the cottage. She goes inside, with some excuse or other. Then I'll come up with some of the neighbours, we'll knock on the door, and pull out the person who comes to the door. That way, neither of the Doyles will get a chance to use a gun, and we can get both Liam *and* Jinny out safely.'

Nobody spoke for a second. Then Harriet said, 'Yes, it's a good plan. All right, shall we go?' and got up.

'Wait,' said Joe suddenly. 'Now *I* have a question. *Why?* You want me to forget about my harvest and put my daughter in danger. But why today? The television reporters are saying that the terrorists won't hurt Liam until Friday. That's what Keith says. So we don't need to hurry.'

'I've told you, if the terrorists don't get what they want by two o'clock *today*, Liam will die.' Harriet stared angrily at Joe.

50

Keith suddenly said, 'I don't think they're really interested in those special homes for children. I think they want something more important.'

'You're right,' said Harriet tiredly. 'They've got publicity for their ideas now, of course. But – I see that I'll have to tell you what they really want. They want to do something that people will remember for a long time. They want to destroy, to *bomb* the most famous family in the country.'

'You mean—' said Bella Slattery. 'But that's *impossible*. The royal family always have police and detectives around them, don't they?'

'You only need one terrorist with a bomb, in the right crowd at the right time. At two o'clock this afternoon,' replied Harriet. 'I was investigating Free People, you see. And when I discovered their plan, they took Liam, to stop me warning the police. It's difficult for me, isn't it? If I warn the police, Free People will kill Liam – and say that he died because his mother, his *family*, chose not to save him. But if I don't warn the police, there will be several deaths in another, more famous family. And Free People will say that they died because of my love for my son, my *family*. Either way, Free People win the game, because the idea of the family gets bad publicity.'

She put her head in her hands and sat very still.

Joe stood up. 'I understand now. We'll help you.'

'But–' said Keith miserably, 'shouldn't we tell the police about the bomb before we start?'

'Yes,' said Harriet. She was finding it difficult to speak. 'I decided yesterday to warn the police. So the royal family are safe. But Liam will be dead after two o'clock, if we don't get him out.'

11.00 a.m.

Doyle had gone out and Tug was washing the breakfast dishes when there was a knock on the door. The Woman hid the guns and opened the door. It was the girl who had come with the policeman.

'Hallo, Mrs Doyle,' the girl said politely. 'We just wanted to invite you to our harvest party this evening. It's very good fun—' She saw Tug in the kitchen and ran through the sitting-room to him. 'Do come, Philip.'

Just then they heard Doyle's car coming very fast up the road. Tug saw sudden fear in the girl's face. The car door banged, and Doyle hurried into the house, shouting orders at the Woman.

'Come on! We've got to leave! Harriet Shakespeare's in the village! I met that stupid little girl from the post office just down the road, and she told me! Bring the boy! And that girl! And the guns and the radio!'

In a few moments they were all in the car, driving fast down the road away from the cottage.

'So what's your plan, Doyle?' asked the Woman. She had her gun in her hand, and was ready to shoot.

'You'll see. We're going somewhere safe for the next two or three hours – Oh no!'

There were four men walking along the road towards

them. Doyle drove faster, straight at them, and at the last moment the men jumped to one side, shouting and banging on the roof of the car. The next minute the car turned away from the village, and up to the moors.

The car finally stopped high up above the valley. 'Get out!' ordered Doyle. 'Start walking!' They walked up the long ridge that Tug had seen from the kitchen window. The wind was strong and cold, and they could see a long way on both sides of the ridge.

'Stop here!' shouted Doyle. 'Now we wait for visitors!' They did not have to wait long. Two cars drove fast up the hill and stopped a few hundred metres away. Tug saw the men who had been on the road, with a boy who was older than him, and – Hank.

At the last moment the men jumped to one side.

53

'Stay there!' shouted Doyle to them. He was holding the girl by her hair, and slowly he put his gun to her head. 'If you come any nearer, I'll shoot!' Then he smiled at Tug and the Woman. 'Sit down, everyone,' he said. 'We're going to wait and listen to the news.'

Why not? thought Tug. It all seemed like a dream. He sat on the grass, staring at the radio.

2.25 p.m.

This is probably the last wind that I'll ever feel, thought Jinny. *When they hear the news, they'll know that their plan has failed. And then they'll shoot us.* She could see the blue uniforms of policemen in the little group of people waiting by the cars. Some policemen had guns. But Doyle and the Hare-woman were very careful to keep the boy and Jinny in front of their own bodies.

'Right,' said Doyle. 'Now let's listen to the two-thirty news. We're waiting to hear of some important deaths. If those people haven't died, you'll know that Harriet Shakespeare chose to save their lives, not her son's. Because he's less important to her than they are.'

The boy's face went white. *It's not true*, Jinny wanted to say, *she loves you! I've seen that!*

They listened silently to the news. At the end, Doyle turned off the radio and said, 'Now, let's talk.'

'What about?' asked the boy in a high, frightened voice. 'You're going to kill me, aren't you?'

'Oh, yes,' said Doyle. 'We're going to kill you. But you

can choose something first. Harriet Shakespeare can't be sure that you're Liam because she's too far away to see you clearly. And if she's not sure, you can't be sure, can you? So I'm going to call her over here. She's going to walk slowly towards us. Then we can see her face when she decides if you are Liam or not.'

'Then you'll shoot me, I suppose?' said the boy.

'No, *I* won't. Your mother will.'

Jinny did not understand why the boy turned to stare at the Hare-woman. 'Ma – would you really shoot me?' he said.

Doyle laughed. 'You don't know her very well, do you? She killed her own baby twelve years ago.'

Nobody spoke for a moment.

'So,' continued Doyle, 'you can wait for Harriet Shakespeare to decide who you are, to put you in a box with a name on it. Or you can choose for yourself, and spend your last moments of life how you want.'

'We're giving you the chance to choose,' added the Hare-woman, almost gently, ' – to choose who you really are, inside yourself.'

Tug tried to think clearly. *Oh Hank! What would you choose?* Suddenly, he could hear her voice in his head. *Do I have to decide everything for you? Decide for yourself!* He smiled. Of course she was his mother! He knew it now, without question. Now it was easy to decide.

He stood up. 'I'm ready,' he said, and began to run away from Hank, along the ridge towards the Castle Rock.

Jinny stared. *Why was he running that way?* she thought. But the Hare-woman was now lifting the gun in her hands, ready to shoot the boy.

'You're crazy!' screamed Jinny. 'Don't shoot him—!'

Doyle's hand suddenly covered her mouth. 'Hurry up,

But the Hare-woman was now lifting the gun in her hands.

you stupid cow,' he said to the Hare-woman, 'or it'll be too late.'

And Jinny could see that the police, the farmers and Harriet were beginning to come nearer. Jinny stared at the Hare-woman. Her face looked desperate, like . . . who was it? Like Harriet Shakespeare, when she arrived at the farmhouse, worried about her son, because she loved him.

Suddenly Jinny bit Doyle's hand hard, and pulled her mouth away. She shouted at the Hare-woman, using the words that her own mother had used to her.

'It's because you love him that you want to kill him! But if you kill him, you'll only destroy yourself!'

The Hare-woman looked round, surprised. At that moment, there was a bang and she put her hand to her side. A policeman had shot her. Doyle ran to take her gun before she fell, but before he could take it, she threw it high up in the air. It fell over the side of the ridge.

'Run, Tug, run! You're free!' she called into the wind.

And Harriet Shakespeare, running towards them, cried at the same moment, 'Tug, it's all right! You're safe!'

Tug heard the sound of the gun, and then the two shouts behind him. But he did not stop, because the only thing that mattered was the running. His legs ached, and his feet hurt, but in front of him was the Castle Rock and he knew that he could reach it. And as he ran, he sang in his head, *This is me. Here I am, Hank. Here I am, Ma. This is me. This is who I am.*

GLOSSARY

beat *(n)*   a sound in music that comes again and again

believe   to think that something is true or right

desperate   having no hope, ready to say or do any wild or
dangerous thing

fold   to bend something (e.g. paper) into a smaller, different
shape

government   the group of people who control the country

hammer *(v)*   to hit something hard (e.g. nails into wood) with a
tool called a hammer

harvest   the time when corn and other farm crops are cut or
picked

investigate   to ask questions and discover what is wrong

Ma   a word for mother that some children use

moors   open, rough land on hills, usually without trees

publicity   doing things that make sure as many people as
possible know about your ideas

rent *(v)*   to pay to use another person's flat or house

revolutionary   wanting complete change

ridge   the long narrow top of a line of hills

royal   of a king or queen

slide (past tense **slid**)   to move quickly and easily downwards

stare   to look at someone or something for a long time

tear (past tense **tore**)   to pull something apart or into pieces

terrorists   very violent people who kill, or promise to kill, other
people if they don't get what they want

throw (past tense **threw**)   to move your arm quickly to send
something through the air

On the Edge

ACTIVITIES

ACTIVITIES

Before Reading

1 **Read the story introduction on the first page of the book, and the back cover. What do you know now about Tug and Jinny? Answer these questions.**

   1 Where is Tug?
   2 Who has put him there?
   3 How does he feel?
   4 Is he sure of his real name?
   5 Who do the Woman and the Man say he is?
   6 What kind of work does Jinny do?
   7 What has she heard at the cottage on the moors?
   8 Why does she do nothing at first?

2 **Can you guess what will happen in this story? Choose Y (Yes) or N (No) for each of these ideas.**

   1 Tug will escape and hide on Jinny's farm. Y/N
   2 Jinny will get into the cottage and help Tug escape. Y/N
   3 Jinny will also be taken prisoner by the Woman and the Man called Doyle. Y/N
   4 The Woman and the Man called Doyle will make Tug help them in a crime. Y/N
   5 Tug will discover that the Woman and the Man called Doyle really are his parents. Y/N
   6 There will be shooting, and someone will die. Y/N
   7 Jinny will save Tug's life. Y/N

ACTIVITIES

While Reading

Read Chapter 1. Who said or thought this? What, or who, were they talking or thinking about?

1 *'I've been trying to do that for weeks!'*
2 'Why should other people do it for you?'
3 'It's too noisy! We can't talk!'
4 'We're in the cottage that we've rented for our holiday . . .'
5 *'Why do you always feel sorry for yourself?'*
6 'How terrible! That poor boy!'
7 'We prefer to do everything for ourselves.'
8 'Philip fell over and crashed into some furniture.'
9 *'Why are you lying?'*

Read Chapter 2, and put these sentences in the right order.

1 Doyle caught her and told her to go away.
2 She began to hit him across the face, again and again.
3 The Woman brought Tug a hot breakfast on a tray.
4 She fell, and slid down the hill to the cottage garden.
5 Then the Man came in and stopped her hitting Tug.
6 The next day Tug threw his paper dart out of the window.
7 Tug heard a girl's voice in the garden and shouted 'Help!'
8 Jinny went to watch the house from some trees on a hill.
9 Jinny told her friend Keith about the shout for help.
10 But the Woman ran in and knocked Tug to the floor.

61

Before you read Chapter 3 (*Free People*), can you guess the answers to these questions?

1 'Free People' is the name of . . .

    a) a group of terrorists.

    b) Harriet Shakespeare's television programme.

2 What happens to Tug's paper dart with his message?

    a) Doyle finds the paper in the garden and burns it.

    b) Jinny finds the paper two days later.

Read Chapter 3. Match these halves of sentences and join them with these linking words.

because / but / but / so / that / when / which / who

1 The terrorists _____ had taken Tug . . .

2 They took Harriet Shakespeare's son . . .

3 Harriet thought that her son, Tug, was in London, . . .

4 _____ the Woman was kind to Tug one night, . . .

5 Jinny and her brother Oz found a message, . . .

6 Mr Hollins and Jinny went to the cottage, . . .

7 Mrs Doyle explained to Mr Hollins . . .

8 During the visit Doyle had a gun in his pocket, . . .

9 _____ Tug had thrown out of the window.

10 _____ their son Philip was like a five-year-old child.

11 wanted everyone to live free from the prison of the family.

12 _____ Tug was too afraid to scream for help.

13 _____ she had investigated them in the past.

14 Tug began to feel she could be his mother.

15 _____ the Doyles seemed just like a family on holiday.

16 _____ in fact he was in the north of England.

Read Chapter 4. Choose the best question-word for these questions, and then answer them.

What / Why

1 . . . did the terrorists want the Government to do?
2 . . . did Jinny realize when she changed the colour of Liam Shakespeare's hair in the photo?
3 . . . did Tug try to remember things about himself?
4 . . . was Doyle so angry about the family Sunday lunch?
5 . . . did Keith suggest doing?
6 . . . did 'Free People' believe wasn't natural?
7 . . . was Doyle angry when he came in with Tug's supper?
8 . . . was Harriet Shakespeare angry with Jinny?

Before you read Chapter 5, try to guess how the story ends. Choose Y (Yes) or N (No) for each idea below.

1 Harriet Shakespeare comes north to look for Tug. Y/N
2 The terrorists get what they wanted. Y/N
3 Jinny helps to save Tug's life. Y/N
4 The Woman is sorry for Tug, and lets him escape. Y/N
5 The police go to the cottage and shoot their way in. Y/N
6 Joe Slattery makes a plan to get Tug out. Y/N
7 Doyle kills Tug, then shoots the Woman and himself. Y/N
8 Doyle and the Woman take Jinny prisoner as well. Y/N
9 Tug falls down Ashdale Great Edge and breaks a leg. Y/N
10 The police shoot one of the terrorists. Y/N
11 The terrorists shoot Harriet Shakespeare. Y/N
12 Tug and Jinny become friends. Y/N

ACTIVITIES

After Reading

1 Here are three short reports from different newspapers. Find the mistakes in each report and correct them.

1 Today the army caught the 'Free Children' terrorists in Derbyshire. Radio reporter Harriet Shakespeare discovered where the terrorists were holding her 30-year-old brother, and the army was called. Both the terrorists were shot. Brother and sister are now back home in Edinburgh.

2 Young Jinny Slattery, daughter of local teacher Joe Slattery, saved Liam Shakespeare's life today. She and Liam were held at gunpoint in a field by a man and a woman. The man was about to shoot Liam, while the woman held Jinny, but Jinny bravely bit her arm and shouted. As the man looked round in surprise, he was shot by Mr Slattery.

3 A plan to shoot the Royal Family has failed, because a reporter warned the Queen in time. The terrorists who planned the shooting had taken the reporter's son from his school, and were holding him in a flat in the west of England. Luckily, the police found the boy, who is safe and well. The police hope to arrest the terrorists soon.

Now choose the best headline for each report.

- PLAN TO BOMB ROYALS
- LOCAL GIRL SAVES BOY'S LIFE
- MOTHER AND SON TOGETHER AGAIN

2 **When the terrorists were arrested, Jinny told the police what she knew. Complete her statement, using as many words as you like.**

On the night the Doyles arrived, I heard _____. The next day I met Mrs Doyle in the post office, and she _____. That seemed strange, so on Tuesday I went up to the cottage, and while I _____, I heard _____. Mr Doyle was very unfriendly so I _____, but on Friday, when my brother Oz and I were _____, we found _____. But then, when Mr Hollins went _____, the Doyles seemed _____, although I was sure that I saw the boy _____. Then I noticed that the boy's blue eyes were the same _____, on Keith's video of the news, and I recognized his face from _____.

3 **Do you agree (A) or disagree (D) with these ideas? Give your reasons.**

1 Ma was not as bad as Doyle because she was sometimes kind to Tug.

2 We have to feel sorry for Ma and Doyle because they came from unhappy families themselves.

3 Harriet was right to warn the police about the bomb, although it meant putting her son's life in danger.

4 Joe Slattery did the right thing when he tried to save Tug's life, although it meant putting his daughter in danger.

5 When terrorists take someone prisoner, they should always get what they ask for.

4 There are 21 words from the story (4 letters or longer) in this word search. Find the words (they go from left to right, and from top to bottom), and draw lines through them.

F	I	O	G	O	V	E	R	N	M	E	N	T	R
G	N	T	E	R	R	O	R	I	S	T	E	P	T
T	V	H	H	E	E	X	C	W	A	R	N	U	I
T	E	F	A	M	I	L	Y	E	C	M	E	B	P
N	S	T	R	E	A	N	M	R	O	Y	A	L	R
D	T	T	V	S	H	D	I	D	T	B	P	I	I
I	I	D	E	S	P	E	R	A	T	E	R	C	S
N	G	K	S	A	H	S	R	R	A	L	E	I	O
F	A	C	T	G	A	T	O	T	G	I	T	T	N
R	T	D	A	E	B	R	R	O	E	E	E	Y	E
U	F	T	T	H	B	O	M	B	E	V	N	I	R
D	E	C	R	A	Z	Y	A	S	H	E	D	G	E

Which 3 words from the word search tell you about the terrorists' *real* plan?

5 Look at the word search again, and write down all the letters without a line through them. Begin with the first line, and go across each line to the end. You should have 44 letters, which will make a sentence of 9 words.

1 What is the sentence, and who said it?
2 Who remembered these words later, and where?
3 Why was it helpful for the person to remember these words, just at that moment?

6 Perhaps Tug and Jinny talked to each other at the end of the story. Put their conversation in the right order, and write in the speakers' names. Tug speaks first (number 3).

1 _____: 'The Hare-Woman? Why do you call her that?'

2 _____: 'Yes, I saw you make the shape of the word with your mouth. But Mr Hollins didn't take it seriously.'

3 _____: 'Did anyone find my message, do you know?'

4 _____: 'Why didn't you call to us for help while we were there?'

5 _____: 'Why not?'

6 _____: 'My brother and I did. We took it to Mr Hollins.'

7 _____: 'I was afraid to. Doyle had a gun in his pocket. But I tried to say the word "help" to you.'

8 _____: 'She looked like a hare, I thought. She was really frightening. She very nearly killed you!'

9 _____: 'And then you and Mr Hollins came up to the cottage, with that story about the lost dog.'

10 _____: 'Because the Hare-Woman had told him you were a bit strange – like a five-year-old child, in fact.'

7 If you ever need to build up a picture of 'the real you', like Tug (see page 38), what can you say about yourself? Think of some different and unusual things to complete this list.

- I like _____
- I hate _____
- I can _____
- I can _____
- I can _____

ABOUT THE AUTHOR

Gillian Clare Cross was born in London, in England, in 1945. She studied at Oxford University, and during this time she met and married her husband. She has been writing since the 1970s, and has also done various jobs, including working in a village bakery and being an assistant to a Member of Parliament. She has four children, and lives near Coventry, in the Midlands.

Gillian Cross has written a large number of popular books for children and young adults. Her stories have many different settings, both historical and modern. *The Iron Way* (1979) is about the building of the railways in the 1840s, while *The Dark Behind the Curtain* (1982) is a ghost story set in a modern school. Other stories with modern settings include *On the Edge* (1984), *Chartbreak* (1986), set in the world of rock music, *New World* (1996), a mystery about a computer game, and *Pictures in the Dark* (1998). She has won several prizes for her writing: the 1990 Carnegie Medal for *Wolf*, and in 1992 the Smarties Prize and the Whitbread Children's Novel Award for *The Great Elephant Chase*. One of her most popular titles is *The Demon Headmaster* (1982); after this came *The Demon Headmaster Series*, which was filmed by BBC Television.

Gillian Cross's stories show how people behave in exciting or difficult situations. Many of her characters, like Tug in *On the Edge*, have to fight battles with themselves as well as with the world, before finding freedom or peace of mind. She tries to show how her stories fit into the wider world we all live in, but above all, she writes, 'I want to entertain, to amuse, and to move my readers.'

ABOUT BOOKWORMS

OXFORD BOOKWORMS LIBRARY
Classics • True Stories • Fantasy & Horror • Human Interest
Crime & Mystery • Thriller & Adventure

The OXFORD BOOKWORMS LIBRARY offers a wide range of original and adapted stories, both classic and modern, which take learners from elementary to advanced level through six carefully graded language stages:

Stage 1 (400 headwords)	**Stage 4** (1400 headwords)
Stage 2 (700 headwords)	**Stage 5** (1800 headwords)
Stage 3 (1000 headwords)	**Stage 6** (2500 headwords)

More than fifty titles are also available on cassette, and there are many titles at Stages 1 to 4 which are specially recommended for younger learners. In addition to the introductions and activities in each Bookworm, resource material includes photocopiable test worksheets and Teacher's Handbooks, which contain advice on running a class library and using cassettes, and the answers for the activities in the books.

Several other series are linked to the OXFORD BOOKWORMS LIBRARY. They range from highly illustrated readers for young learners, to playscripts, non-fiction readers, and unsimplified texts for advanced learners.

Oxford Bookworms Starters	*Oxford Bookworms Factfiles*
Oxford Bookworms Playscripts	*Oxford Bookworms Collection*

Details of these series and a full list of all titles in the OXFORD BOOKWORMS LIBRARY can be found in the *Oxford English* catalogues. A selection of titles from the OXFORD BOOKWORMS LIBRARY can be found on the next pages.

The Crown of Violet

GEOFFREY TREASE

Retold by John Escott

High up on a stone seat in the great open-air theatre of Athens, Alexis, son of Leon, watches the Festival of Plays – and dreams of seeing his own play on that famous stage.

So, as the summer passes, Alexis writes his play for the next year's Festival. But then, with his friend Corinna, he learns that Athens has enemies – enemies who do not like Athenian democracy, and who are planning a revolution to end it all . . .

Kidnapped

ROBERT LOUIS STEVENSON

Retold by Clare West

'I ran to the side of the ship. "Help, help! Murder!" I screamed, and my uncle slowly turned to look at me. I did not see any more. Already strong hands were pulling me away. Then something hit my head; I saw a great flash of fire, and fell to the ground . . .'

And so begin David Balfour's adventures. He is kidnapped, taken to sea, and meets many dangers. He also meets a friend, Alan Breck. But Alan is in danger himself, on the run from the English army across the wild Highlands of Scotland . . .

Moondial

HELEN CRESSWELL

Retold by John Escott

'Moondial!' As Minty spoke the word, a cold wind went past her, and her ears were filled with a thousand frightened voices. She shut her eyes and put her hands over her ears – and the voices and the wind went away. Minty opened her eyes . . . *and knew that she was in a different morning, not the one she had woken up to.*

And so Minty's strange adventure begins – a journey through time into the past, where she finds Tom, and Sarah . . . and the evil Miss Vole.

The Railway Children

EDITH NESBIT

Retold by John Escott

'We have to leave our house in London,' Mother said to the children. 'We're going to live in the country, in a little house near a railway line.'

And so begins a new life for Roberta, Peter, and Phyllis. They become the railway children – they know all the trains, Perks the station porter is their best friend, and they have many adventures on the railway line.

But why has their father had to go away? Where is he, and will he ever come back?

'Who, Sir? Me, Sir?'

K. M. PEYTON

Retold by Diane Mowat

Sam Sylvester is a teacher who wants his class to have ambition, and to do great things in life. So he enters them for a sporting competition against the rich students of Greycoats School.

The team that he has chosen for the competition think Sam has gone crazy. 'Who, Sir? Me, Sir?' says little Hoomey, his eyes round with horror. 'We'll never beat Greycoats,' the others cry. 'Never in a million years!'

But you don't know what you can do – until you try . . .

The Whispering Knights

PENELOPE LIVELY

Retold by Clare West

'I don't know that you have done anything wrong,' Miss Hepplewhite said. 'But it is possible that you have done something rather dangerous.'

William and Susie thought they were just playing a game when they cooked a witch's brew in the old barn and said a spell over it, but Martha was not so sure. And indeed, the three friends soon learn that they have called up something dark and evil out of the distant past . . .